The Loss Detector

A Novella-in-Flash

Meg Pokrass

BAMBOO DART PRESS

LOS ANGELES † NEW YORK † LONDON † SYDNEY

The Loss Detector by Meg Pokrass

ISBN: 978-1-947240-03-2

eISBN: 978-1-947240-04-9

First Printing 2020

"The Big Dipper", originally published in the collection *Damn Sure Right* (Press 53) and in *Fractured Lit*

"The Bug Man", originally published in *Tin House* and in the collection *Alligators At Night* (Ad Hoc Fiction)

"Perfecto", a version of this story was published in *Storysouth* as "Rollerskating, Barking"

For information:

Bamboo Dart Press

chapbooks@bamboodartpress.com

Curated and operated by Dennis Callaci and Mark Givens

Bamboo Dart Press 001

www.pelekinesis.com

www.bamboodartpress.com

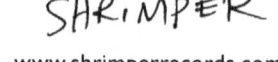
www.shrimperrecords.com

Contents

For Sian and Hannah

*"We have the wacky mode. Why do we have the wacky mode?
To break their hearts."* —Donald Barthelme

Dad's Ears

Dad's ears looked kind. Gentle. Small. He didn't like them, said they emasculated him. Ma said he was right. "He has moon-shaped ears," she said, "but please don't ever repeat this. He can't laugh about it."

Nothing about him seemed to work the way it should. With such small ears, how did he hear everything we said in private? When me and Josh whispered about running away, he'd say, a day or two later, "How about you kids go study the intelligence of pigeons? Pigeons try to fly, but they really can't. That's why you see them squashed in the road."

I wanted to name myself after a movie star, someone mighty and good, someone everyone liked. I thought about it, then asked Josh. As usual, he was nibbling on a carrot, pretending to be a rabbit.

"I like *Meryl Streep*," I said.

"That's just about right."

Ma kept saying she was gaining weight. "Look at these bingo wings, kids," she'd say. "She wants to be sexy," Josh said. "Maybe she's tired of being a mother."

She was a mystery to us in many ways, but she had large ears. Ears you could trust.

For the next few months, until the three of us left Dad in the middle of the night, my brother called me Streep. Ma would bring us mint leaf lemonade, and we'd sit in the back yard trying to be kids who were pleasant to be with, who didn't notice ears, who smiled like movie stars.

Villa Monterey Apartments

In California the earth shakes. Ma says this when we cross from Nevada into California. She pushes the gas pedal hard, and the car jumps. Josh and I clap.

Today Ma's meeting with a realty company, so we get to stay at Tessa's Hollywood apartment with a pool. Tessa's twelve years older than me and nine years older than Josh. She has a bronzed face, streaked hair. Her boyfriend, West, smiles at me. Dark muscles, swimming shorts, Popeye shoulders stretching out against her avocado shag rug. He just landed a part in a TV show. Josh bounces off the walls. Tessa makes sure he hangs out by the pool all day.

"Can you step on my back right here, Nikki?" West asks.

Dad always seemed old and hurt—I hurt Dad by being so little and clumsy. Once he taught me a lesson, I never bothered him again. West doesn't know how bad Josh and me are.

Tessa won't talk about Dad. Josh says pretend we never knew him.

"She's not to get hurt!" Tessa barks—a hundred years crawling into her voice.

"She's not a baby," Josh tells her, blowing air, making horse-lips.

Stepping on West's back feels soft, hard, squishy—all at once. Maybe like an earthquake?

"You win," Tessa says. "You three fucking win."

Tessa acts a lot older than when she left Pennsylvania to study acting in Los Angeles. She walks out swishing a bright-red towel behind her.

"Feet can't hurt anyone," Josh says.

* * *

In the pool, Tessa and West don't talk, just touch each other's faces bobbing up and down like otters in the deep end. Josh floats around the edges on a raft. We could be in a movie. Seven short palm trees stand in a line behind the pool deck waiting for autographs.

Ma told me smog is invisible once you're in it. Everything sparkles in California: the VACANCY sign on the apartment building, West's frog goggles, the two lines of pool water slipping from Josh's red eyes.

We Could Have Landed Anywhere

Ma drives to Goodwill and finds herself two bright dresses. We're starting all over. She's going to sell houses in California, like she did before. We have to have our car shampooed and blow-dried. She'll be driving nice, rich strangers around to see properties.

So many bugs juiced themselves to death on the car, it's like weird brown pie-crust around the windows. Ma pours herself a glass of wine, kicks off her shoes.

"Bug suicide," Josh says.

We eat burritos. Ma sleeps in the kitchen nook. Me and Josh get two squashed bedrooms upstairs.

When the Santa Ana winds come up at night, we run outside in our t-shirts, hypnotized by the feeling of bare feet on warm stone. The stones are green and eggshell-white with see-through lines through them like highways. Ma says this means there is crystal inside. Josh dances wildly, swinging a butterfly net.

The smell of jasmine flowers at night makes us feel drunk. "What's that heavenly smell?" Ma says, pretending to swoon.

Will We Marry Him?

Grant is Ma's real estate partner, very tall, nice to us. He teaches me and Josh how to dry our backs properly, holding an invisible towel.

He and Ma steal out for long lunches, sharing meatball sandwiches. Ma has her hair frosted.

"Will we marry him?"

"Noooo," she clucks her tongue at me. "He's ten years too young for me. Besides, he's engaged."

Grant lets me feel his face when he gives me piggyback rides. Thick black hair, bushy eyebrows. We take weekend picnics at the beach. When catsup blows off the hotdog buns, we all laugh.

He and Ma are selling houses like crazy, a great team. Already they've brought home an award. We place it on our mantel.

Josh and me want a pet, so Grant builds us a rabbit hutch. Ma buys a bunny from the pet store—white with black spots, shocked eyes. But the bunny won't let us pick her up.

Near Christmas, I see Ma and Grant near her car, leaning in—Grant holding her cheeks and letting go. Ma making small animal sounds.

She stares at the ground hard, as though something has fallen. She sways.

* * *

A few weeks later, Grant brings his fiancée, Jane, by for eggnog. Ma dresses real nice, but she can't outdo Jane. Younger and blond with magenta lips and outlined eyes.

Later that night, Ma falls asleep with the TV on. Josh and I slip outside barefoot. Crickets like crazy, but no car sounds. He opens the rabbit hutch to set it free.

"Good luck, good luck!" we say, waving goodbye.

Miracle

Ma locks her bedroom door, stays in there with the TV on. She only comes out once in the late afternoon, to defrost dinner. Josh and I suck on salty pretzels all afternoon. We don't know what to do, so we dust the furniture.

Tessa calls on the phone and says, "Fuck him!" She says Ma was in love with Grant. She says he led her on and used her. I can't believe that's true. But I stop listening, latching on to the mesmerizing sound of the word "Fuck!" I want to burst into Ma's room and yell "Fuck!" To make her look at me, like she did when I was little. I want her to see me clearly again, like I'm her miracle.

Stand Back

"Stand back!" Ma says, striking a match, lighting the old Wedgwood stove. Whoosh! like the end of the world.

"Omelets from scraps are keen," she says, sucking a cigarette. Button mushrooms for eyes, red onion slices into tight smiles.

Tessa's hair almost completely obscures her face. Despite some good parts, she has also lost a few good roles and says she needs to take a break. She shivers like a skinny dog when the fog comes in.

Sometimes Josh or I will poke through her hair, whispering, "How much for your last three bites?"

"A million and a car," she'll say.

Ma can even make cow's tongue lovely. She cooks better than anyone.

Tessa excuses herself for the bathroom. Josh and I look at each other while the sink hisses, singing with the angry toilet, but the sound of her coughs travels. We pass the time by playing Two Truths and a Lie.

Our Sloppy Stay Here

Ma's *To Read* stack is shrinking. She lies in bed on black fuzzy pillows, her nightgown buttoned up to her throat, reading furiously. She says there are years of good books she's missed.

I'm making a Christmas list, trying to think of gifts that don't cost a fortune—like a key chain for Josh. He wants things that fart. I can pick some things up at the gas station by the school.

Josh is planning to get Ma Travel Monopoly, even though we don't travel. I tell him good luck finding one.

He says he will, it's not my problem—and that we'll be able to play with her even when she's staying in her room. It has been at least a year since we played a game together.

He's looking for the limited edition.

I wonder what it would be like to live on a different planet and just come back to Earth occasionally. For a week or so I could stop worrying about Ma drinking. She says our planet will soon go up in a blaze. Earth is losing the long, shitty game of marriage to humans.

"Hey, we've really loved our sloppy stay here!" she says.

Zorro, Dog-Criminal

Zorro is a mutt. Ma says mostly retriever. I call him my boyfriend, put hats on him. Josh says Zorro acts gay.

Fleas bite our ankles. We pile eucalyptus branches thick under the beds to scare the fleas away, but it doesn't work.

On my way outside to feed the turtle I almost trip on a turtle shell. I run inside. Zorro is gnawing at the itch on his butt. "Bad dog!" This is the third dead turtle.

Itching too, I'm ready to tear my own skin off. I picture the empty shell, and a shiver gets stuck inside my brain.

I wonder how much longer we'll live here. These days Ma goes on about how much Zorro costs us with all his problems. His itches. How many times he has ruined the screen door trying to get inside when we're gone. She calls him a home wrecker. He backs himself into a corner near the aprons, breathing hard and making friends with the wall.

Aliens

After martinis at night, Ma's sure she's seen a spaceship touch down twice in the side yard by the fruit trees. Twice. Or more! she says.

Mornings there's no sign of alien life. Transporting oranges in my pockets, I climb the oak tree and plant myself on the flattest branch to scout for invaders.

What I see: weeds invading the ice plant, yellow patches of grass multiplying in circles where Zorro pees, trees dropping brown, useless fruit. Nothing seems to be blooming.

I search for signs of otherworldly visitation. No luck.

The Bug Man

One morning, reading the paper in the kitchen, Ma yells, "SHIT!"

Now what? I wonder. Ants in the kitchen again? Dog crap near the sink?

"Look at this obit! I wondered where he'd been!"

Ma always says we're lucky people, because the bug man comes over to our house for free, squirts insecticide in places nobody has ever seen.

He has a large termite sculpture on his truck. Ma's real estate company gives him lots of business. He smiles at me.

At Christmas, he surrounds Ma with his long arms, a hug of appreciation. Our secret hope is that somehow the bug man will take us to a place with plush carpets, no bugs.

"Cancer, like his father who started the goddamn business!" she says.

I hate that word—cancer. Ma looks ugly and old, saying it, like a woman with a seed stuck in her teeth. Josh runs outside, and I hear the clatter of his skateboard. She asks me to clip out his obit, as though he'd belonged to us.

Thank You

Ma does not frost her hair anymore or wear bright colors. Vain people make a habit of working on their looks, she says. But a mother—

A mother goes to work every day of the week.

A mother has ethics.

A mother is an honest person.

A banner—*good citizen*—rises like a For-Sale sign from Ma's caving brow.

She prides herself on being an "ethical realtor." Sometimes she works seven days a week, from eight in the morning until eight at night. She gets a mug at Christmas from the company that says *Thank You*.

The Look of Combinations

The curvy cool girls eat lunch in a flock. The skinny sports girls perform cartwheels and flips.

When Lila and I walk home from school, I confess that I'm in love with Peter.

"Peter Doyle?"

"Yep!"

Peter looks like he belongs to the beach, like moonstones or fan shells. I ride my bike past his house, and a shiver wraps around my hips.

"At least, I think he's nice," I say to Lila, tying my hair into a fountain knot on top of my head.

She laughs, slaps her skinny tan knees at the thought that I like cute boys and expect them to like me back.

In my school notebook I write Peter Doyle's name in cursive, let it fly around my own name, testing the look of combinations. At home I collect photos of swallowtails and other exotic butterflies, especially from Africa. I imagine the lanky arms of Peter Doyle, his elbows flapping toward my house. One day he'll land on me.

Criminal Brother

"Your brother is in trouble again," Ma says. Her gig in life these days is to tell me about my criminal brother.

"My freaking God, how tricky that boy is," she says with a slur, pouring a glass of wine while trying to read the paper.

Something or someone is always interrupting her. The phone, or defrosted meat, or the dog trying to break down the fence.

"Your sister is dangerously slim," she says, "but at least she's not sneaky."

I'm nibbling popcorn to try to get thin, and watching a TV show where someone's sad, senile mother-in-law is yelling at the neighbor's wife and making a scene of herself. Wearing only her slippers and underwear. Why would anyone bother to get old and become a relic? That's what it all comes down to—walking around like a zombie.

I hear a fluttery sound from upstairs. My brother shuffles down in a huff, running his hands through his chalky hair, looking like he just woke up for the third time today.

"Joshua, your teacher wants to speak with me about your antics at school," she says.

"Ma, this is an invention. Please tell her to fuck herself," he says.

Ma sits down and looks at my brother. She has a sad and sloppy expression. We kids and our disastrous dog are aging her. Soon enough she'll be demented, walking around the neighborhood forgetting which house is ours.

"If we don't deal with this, it's just going to fester," she says as if I'm her partner, ready for battle, though it's hard to know whose side she wants me to be on.

Toast

It's hell trying to get Josh to crack a smile. If he keeps ditching school like this, Ma says, he will be toast. His third school in two years.

He tells me, "I'm a darting asshole."

"Who says that?" I ask.

"Everybody."

I call them stupid fuckers—the idiots who don't give him respect.

I want to say she's crazy, this girl from drama class he crawls behind.

His hair's shiny and gold, I envy it, I like to brush it. That night we watch Masterpiece Theater, acting like old people again, eating brownies, me loving his hair.

How We Calm Ourselves

Josh and me are looking at the weather report—boring as hell here in perfect-land. We wish for bad weather, but it just won't happen.

As usual, I have popcorn stuck in my braces. I feel awkward standing so close to him now that I know he's a burglar. I mean, he steals little doodads from the stores and then shoves them all in his bedroom closet.

I don't steal yet, but I want to. Especially when I pass the perfume bottles, the kind that would make me smell special and lucky.

In my room, I construct a miniature theater out of the bottoms of boxes. I'm not really sure how I want the mother in my play to look, though certainly not old like Ma. I think of actresses I'd like to have play her. Tessa would be too young and skinny, so I rule her out. I sit there, making lists of motherly actresses.

There'd be a romantic scene in a beauty salon, the mother's hair colored a deep mahogany red, her scalp massaged by a professional stylist. I conjure the stylist's face, his attention to detail. The way he'll look at the mother. He loves unusual kids and rescues flawed animals. He becomes her boyfriend.

The Big Dipper

The plastic pool is four feet deep and came from Target, half off. We can float on our backs and think, "Fun times are here," because at least we're not burning hot.

Ma and I watch it fill up with hose water. She looks around the backyard, the neglected trees, and says, "I've got to call those idiots and make sure they get a gardener." Rotting fruit and dog poop.

I'm not going to worry about anything. I'll just float on my back, weightless in my bikini. I suck on the flea bite in the crook of my arm.

The pool and I will make new friends. I'm getting sick of Lila and Blythe. Difficult. Blythe's head looks like Pinocchio's. A violin prodigy with a modern hair cut—short, black, severe. And breasts, adult size, her pride.

I don't really have anything up there yet. Ma says not to worry, but I do. Does late development means small breasts? Ma says no, that she had been the same. "Worth the wait," she says with a wink.

In the new pool, I can float on my back in the dark, looking at the stars. My dream.

Since there is no one else yet, I invite Lila and Blythe for Saturday. Lila can't come because her family's driving to Oxnard. Blythe says, "Sure as heck. I'm all about nighttime and pools and stargazing."

* * *

"Show me the Big Dipper, Nikki," Blythe says. "I want to make sure I know which one it is."

She's wearing her bikini bottoms, but her top is on the side of the pool. The pool feels much smaller with her beside me. I'm glad it was cheap.

I miss Lila's cigarettes. And Lila.

I point up to where I spotted the Big Dipper.

"Uh huh," she says. "A long bent ladle, right?"

She's all wet and slick, with gleaming, womanly breasts. I'm angry at her for taking her top off.

"It looks like a crooked dick," I say. The pool is a bee cemetery. I scoop two up and throw them out. "I don't even really know what a ladle looks like," I say.

All the neighborhood dogs are talking to each other. A bee could be marching down my arm. Something keeps tickling.

"You know what a crooked dick looks like, Nikki?" Blythe says. Her face is large, or maybe it's the moon.

"Not exactly," I say, trying not to let my eyes get caught on her chest, "But I've seen them, and they all have different shapes."

I have a subscription to *Playgirl*. Ma gave it to me for Christmas instead of a new bike. Nothing seems to freak her out, as long as she has two martinis after work.

"So, like… Whose?" Blythe asks.

"I haven't seen that many dicks, but I have…" If I tell her I have a subscription to *Playgirl*, she'll tell everyone. The water gets cooler. The smell of plastic makes things worse. I hope she hasn't peed here, though I would not put it past her.

Playing the Chicken

Dante, our middle school acting teacher, has cast me as a chicken in the final yearly production. This makes me feel lumpy, short, and invisible. Playing a chicken feels like being disliked.

Blonde, giggly Melinda gets the leading role. He casts all the best roles with kids who squeal when he walks into class. They all have light hair. I have dark hair and a curved nose.

Melinda is the most motivated. She jumps up and grabs his ponytail, thrusting out her non-existent tits and narrowing her pool-blue eyes. I try to hide my disappointment, but I feel myself sulking.

"This character is not just a chicken," Dante says. "It is a counterintuitive symbol of hope."

When the class first started, I loved Dante. He was nice to me. He'd lift me up and plop me down and lift me up again because I was so light.

But these days he asks how Tessa's career is going, and I don't understand the details he wants. He asks the name of her agent, and I shrug. My face goes red.

"Tell her I'm her biggest fan," Dante says.

Josh says I should not have to play a chicken at all—and that even if pink feathers look attractive on me and bring out my skin-tone, it's ultimately unfair.

"Symbol of hope, my ass," my Josh says. He tells me to stand up to Dante. To refuse.

At the first read-through, I tell Dante that my sister says hi and thinks I should play a human, even if it's the village idiot or a gnome.

He says, "I'll tell you what. Invite her here to watch the next rehearsal, and we'll figure something out. Maybe she'll teach us some stuff."

When I tell Josh, he says, "No fucking way! That's bribery."

I remind him that a chicken has a past and lots of motivation. I tell him that it will be a fun challenge, even though I really don't think so.

Ma, as usual, doesn't notice anything. She's working or sleeping all the time now and can't be bothered. She hates the world for warming up, dislikes the dog, and blames expensive California life for making her crazy. Being cast as a chicken? Not even worth thinking about.

Hemophilia

Ma's silent smiles are the worst. She wears her "I'm a hemophiliac" pendant all the time now. Zorro scoots back a bit and gets out of her way, just like me and Josh. How do dogs know? He sits at the window every afternoon, waiting for something.

The tip of my nose itches, but I refuse to scratch. The ground's unstable because so little has been done around the house. Spiders bubble up through the floorboards now that the Bug Man has died. Zorro chases spiders and eats some of them. But even he's afraid of the big ones.

These days Josh lives in a brown felt hat. I don't know who gave it to him, but one day he comes home with it on his head and doesn't take it off even when he sleeps.

"Do you have to wear that every minute of every day and night?"

"I'm protecting my brain from spiders."

When I was twelve, afraid of street people, Josh said, "Imagine you're covered in Saran Wrap when you walk past them, and you can't spoil."

I still walk past street people just like that— tight, held in place.

Water Gun

Josh has been expelled from two schools now for peeing in public areas, ditching classes, and failing. Cutting my toenails with the cuticle scissors, he claims he has a millionaire's mind. He collects my clippings in a cup and saves them.

He also promises that when I grow up, my grin will be even. I don't think he's smart enough to know this, but I hide my doubt. My wrists are tiny as a doll's. Worse than Tessa's, he says. Sometimes I hear him slam his door just to get Ma to come downstairs and use her feet in the kitchen and cook for us.

Josh doesn't notice pretty girls, and I wonder if he's hiding something.

I try not to furrow my brow because it makes me ugly. Josh makes a rude gesture when a boy walks by and looks at me. This happens more and more often. Sometimes one of them calls on the phone.

"The climate is changing," Josh cries one night, carving invisible warts out of his foot. Bleeding, he hops around on one foot and tells me to spray him with his water gun. I tell him to stop, and I call for Ma. I'm not afraid of blood.

Blonde

Tessa always brings a pile of *Vogue*s and scatters them like seed when she visits. She's a blonde now. Worried that her hair looks damaged, she douses it in olive oil and applies heat treatments.

"Nothing's ever good enough for Hollywood," Ma says, chucking out old musty pillowcases. Her goal this spring, she says, is to clean the fuck out of the place and to get rid of spore spots.

"Jack shit!" Tessa shrieks from the bathroom. "My fucking roots are black again!"

Ma says, "Let's boils some eggs and do a nice egg salad."

I check the date on the eggs while Ma pulls out the mayonnaise and two glass bowls.

"The kernel of the problem is not with her hair," Ma whispers, starting water to boil.

Vampire

Josh says any kid who calls me *vampire*, especially now that my teeth are fixed, gets punished. "They just want you to notice them," he says. "Those losers think you're hot."

I say, "This isn't worth getting pissy over, Josh. You've already been kicked out of two schools, so leave it alone! How fucking self-destructive do you want to be?"

His hands are twisting and untwisting as if he's envisioning some kid's face he's reshaping. The thought of Josh in a physical fight is some kind of comedy. He's brave, but scrawny, sarcastic, and not the type for physical confrontation.

Slurping noodles at an alarming pace, he practices what he'll say: "You're so into Nikki that your poor widdle balls are wilting. Your little sad-assed dick has died from all that love you give it."

"God!" I say.

"You call her *ugly*. Yeah, right!" he goes on. "So you can make her notice you, so you can make your spermy little mark. Nikki doesn't see you, and you don't like that. Face it, asshole."

I feel nauseous. Josh's face is purple.

"You want her and can't have her! Admit it. You want her to look at you like doom. You love her, everything about her, even her platform shoes that will walk all over your ass."

He is shaking hard. He wears a turquoise chastity ring. He says he plans to remain faithful, but he doesn't say who to. The ring falls off his skinny finger. I've found it dozens of times. He calls me his loss detector. And starts shaking.

What We Want to Be

When adults ask what we want to be when we grow up, I say, "A religious leader," so they'll leave me alone. Sometime, I'll give them *mortician*.

"I'd like to make dead people look better," I say to myself in the mirror.

I want to be an actress like Tessa, of course.

Josh says he wants to be a road-kill scraper, which shuts them up completely.

Sudden Changes

Ma laughs, walking in with her boyfriend Max, arms outstretched.

"Back in Pennsylvania, Nikki tried to stab me once," Ma trills, blushing like a teenager. "Come to Mommy, my little Hun!"

"Ma, I was holding a plastic fork, and I was three years old!" I say.

Max looks at me with false sympathy.

Her hair is ironed now, silky and short. Her face has become unfrozen, her *good citizen* banner taken down. She buys shape-wear and has quit taking medicine for depression. Something is working, coloring her up. She walks on the beach every morning. She says sometimes she misses Pennsylvania, but then she remembers the sea. This makes me angry. The way she loves California, and then hates it for being so great. She colors and outlines her lips for him.

Max.

Middle-Aged Dog Training

Max and Zorro are engaging in middle-aged dog training in the living room. "Do you remember what I said to you about midlife dogs?" Max says to Ma.

"I'm waiting for the drum roll," she says.

I've got a vague memory about it, but it's in the mental compost. Relief is getting quickly rid of whatever Max says, idiotic ideas that subside and are soon replaced by others. He clearly wants me to remember everything he says. His face gets all babyish and indented. For a man who boasts about his truck engine, he really gets nuclear dents.

"A dog must be given confidence, exactly like a child," Max says.

He looks at Ma first, then at me. It's too late for Zorro to learn new tricks.

Ma burps. A rarity. She apologizes, explaining she has been sipping her beer too fast and she's having a relaxing evening, seeing how productive things can get here.

"How much can be done with a flawed, flea-ridden, middle-aged dog?" I say.

"Don't insult Zorro, Nikki. He can understand that!" Max says. "AND he needs a haircut tonight!" He points directly at me. "Ms. Nikki, are you game for the job? I will pay you five dollars to make this middle-aged dog less matted."

Ma says, "And I'll chip in five more!"

Max is drunk, Ma is drunk. I think I should be drunk too.

Fatigue

Ma tells Josh that he has a diagnosis, what the psychiatrist calls "a malaise." Also "oppositional OCD."

She took him to see the psychiatrist because of the strange things he was doing that got him kicked out of his schools. She didn't know where else to turn. She is tired of him failing, she says. He was born with good brains. Max thinks if Josh gets help, he can stop sabotaging himself. He's encouraging this.

"Honey, you strain things in your world," she tells him.

"Mercy, mercy, Lawd have mercy," Josh sings, picking his knee scabs and tapping his feet on the floor—the right one, then the left, then the right and then the left.

Ma says a lot would get better if his feet would just stay still.

"Josh has a marvelously destitute spirit," I say.

"Can somebody pry me free of this?" Ma says.

She claims stress is making her sick. She keeps eating submarine sandwiches and chocolate ice cream, she says, just to make us laugh. "In the last few months I've gained ten pounds." She puffs out her cheeks.

Josh wants to run away before anything really bad happens. He tells me this when we cuddle on the sofa, which we have almost stopped doing.

He doesn't want to watch life happen like this, he says. I know what he means, but I never see it the way he does. The stakes never feel as high to me.

Everything annoys him, he says. He says I am the one thing

that doesn't annoy him, and that annoys him the most.

* * *

"Babushka, I have reserved you for the Parlor Works."

"The mud mask treatment?"

"Yes, the whole summer package," he says.

Josh likes to manicure and pedicure me. I like it because it stops him from pulling the skin off his upper lip. He does a good job too.

By the time he finishes, the chaise lounge will be covered with my nail clippings, and he'll make me leave the room while he collects them. He says something bad will happen if we throw away pieces of ourselves. It's a risk we can't take.

Roof Birthday

We sip Diet Cokes on the roof. Josh says he'd rather have whiskey. It's his birthday. The screen door is open, and we hear Ma watching the news.

I hear the highway's hum, the drag and flap of trucks ruining our sliver of ozone. I'll bet Bob Dylan would write a great song about the world tonight. If I were driving somewhere with him, vacant motels would glow. I tell Josh to tell me what Bob would write and sing.

My elbows hurt from leaning back on the tiles. If someone saw us up here, they'd say, "They're just joking up there, those kids," or maybe scream, "Somebody get them the fuck down!"

A spider crawls over Josh's bare knee. It talks. That is, Josh says he hears it.

"Get that thing off your leg."

He says the spider says, "If you were more understanding, Ma would not be so tired all the time. We could still make her laugh."

Next week he leaves for a disciplinary boarding school in Canada. He says that he won't stay, that he'll find a way out. I ask Josh if I can stay on the roof with him all night. I tell him there's nothing to be afraid of.

White Dreams

"This is not forever," Ma says.

I wonder if Josh has white dreams—the kind someone has right before they get taken away.

Sunrise

A wedge of moonlight sneaks in, and I slip through the back door. Ma and Max are asleep, dreaming their insipid dreams. It's dark outside, but the night sky is clear. A girl can feel safe holding herself inside. There aren't many murders in this town, just one recently, a woman driving up before dawn to the 24-hour pharmacy, a man in the parking lot with wire. That was all I wanted to know.

With Zorro next to me, we trundle downhill toward the beach. My plan is to sit on the sand all night and to think about how to get my brother back. I have my pot with me, and the air feels clear and truthful. With no noise around, no spiders to make up stories, the sand will feel just right on my legs, cool and nest-like.

At the edge of the continent, this place where we live, a small family like ours has little chance of survival. I think of that boy who doesn't look at me, Peter Doyle, how he surfs before school starts. The eye inside my brain sees him riding to the beach before sunrise. That's where he'll find us, right here waiting, Zorro and me, camped out like derelicts in the sand. "Hello there, good morning," I'll say. Wondering if, as usual, he'll look out at the Channel Islands instead of my face.

"Besides, what would a boy like him do with all this beauty?" I ask Zorro. Zorro has no idea that I'm joking. He looks worried. I can see that, even in the pitch black night. So I shine the flashlight over the pavement, to show him it's okay. Just him and me here on Planet Earth, walking to the beach. Where we belong.

When Ma wakes up to an empty house she'll probably fill her

glass and get going early.

I imagine her belly expanding with a child, the way the pockets under her eyes have taken hold. But she's way too old, I tell myself in an even voice. Just the way Josh would say it, with his inflection.

We are almost to the beach now, we can hear the sound of waves, and something else too—something that sounds like empty little shells clinking against each other, trying to stay in one piece as they're flung against the sand.

Perfecto

Lila invites me to spend the night. I'm trying not to fall asleep on her couch, watching *The Late, Late Show*, when she finally lets me know what happened.

She's walking home from school on Thursday, right along Via Esperanza. She hears a horn, turns, and this guy in a car is staring at her, asking, "Where is Las Palmas Drive?" She points the other way, but he just keeps on smiling.

He probably smiled because Lila has plump movie-star lips. Five foot four. Platform shoes. Hair the color of dirty lemons, thick and long, just wavy. Her eyes are green, like those marbles you don't want to lose.

"So, what happens?" I ask I light up a cigarette from her mother's pack. The living room reeks of cat pee, and smoke helps block it out. Lately, I've decided I don't want to smell clean.

"Then he says his brother will give me a ride home."

This she reports like a celebrity, her lips swollen with victory. There seems to be more, and it's waking me up.

"So what's his name?" I ask.

"Perfecto."

She says he gave her a present. Runs to get it from her bedroom. As she flies down the hall, long hair bounces off her butt.

She's back, holding a toilet paper wad. She opens it carefully and pinches out a tiny, hand-rolled joint. We both stare at it, and Lila begins to laugh.

Later, we race into the kitchen to make brownies from a box.

As usual, we eat half of the batter raw. Not long after, I get a stomachache, lie down in a fetal curl.

Later still, chasing each other around the front yard, listening to the neighborhood dogs barking. We're barking back at them— her idea. She says we can trick them into thinking we're dogs.

One of them is Zorro, barking madly from our yard. I can tell it's him by his hoarse, pitiful bark.

Occasionally, he howls, which sounds great—like it's finally coming out of the right part of his body.

Dancing Fool

"I just told Max to chill, Honey. And he's already shacking up with some belly-dancing waitress," Ma says. She's busted her collarbone. How? Trying to ride a bike again, borrowing mine, trying to be the way she was a million years ago. In shape.

She's given up smoking, drinking. Her hair's darkening up. I almost like the new look, but it's not the Ma that Tessa and I have become used to. The one with tipped blond hair and perfumed pits.

"What's wrong with my tail?" Mom says, trying on jeans at least two sizes too small.

"Can you please explain to me what is wrong with my ass?" she repeats, looking into her phone, turned away from the mirror, videoing her ass as she paces back and forth like a wind-up toy. And then she starts to dance.

"Busted!" she sighs, sitting down and exhaling air like a radiator. "Every part of me is middle-aged."

I sit down next to her, peeling a tangerine. I don't want to feed her worry about how she looks. I'm only a kid. How the fuck would I know what's wrong with her ass?

"It was all a bit useless with Max," she says.

"It's simple, Ma," I say, and she looks at me as if she thinks I know exactly how she appears to the rest of the world.

Nothing in our house is bolted down, the way it should be. I look around the living room. Nothing is safe from earthquakes.

"We still need a pilot for this plane, don't we?" she says.

White Wolves

There's a tall man who brings his hybrid wolves to the dog park. In the mirror at home I look like I could use a necklace.

At the movies, I cry at all the parts nobody else thinks are sad. It's a lot like being in the corner of your own life and watching what's sad, or wrong, or what could have been better.

I don't feel alone when I'm alone, but when I'm with others. More alone. The man with the wolves—he doesn't seem alone at all. He often tries to explain his wolves to people while they look them over with squinty glares.

I walk three laps of the dog park before I head home. I wave at the wolf man.

Most evenings I watch for moths under the porch light. I try to save one. Just one. I would own a white wolf if I weren't afraid. There was a womb that kept us inside and then projected us out like flying starfish. We are born into the temptation of white wolves. None of this feels unimportant. The stakes are high.

Sometimes I wear Ma's fake fur so I can feel like a secret animal. This isn't impossible at all.

Planet Earth

Me and Blythe are tanning on bright red beach towels on the sand at Hendri's beach. This time I don't let my mind worry too much about Blythe's exhibitionism. I've overcome my shyness, and we both have our bikini tops off. They lie next to us like sleeping rabbits.

Sometimes there's a language in her eyes that freezes me, but my goal is to become less uptight. Mellow. We're thirteen, and only one of us has an attractive face. The other's got an attractive body. My body has potential, Ma says, but there is no way to know if things will get kinetic.

Riding around in her brother's truck, me and Blythe make weekend plans. We whisper in the back seat while he drives. We call him Jeeves. We hate his jokes. Sometimes he flips us off in the rear view mirror. But today, on the sand, it's all about us. No assholes to fuck with us here. Her eyes are grey, I realize, not black. My eyes are so blue they make people glad they know me. Lately this has become inconvenient, and I wish mine were dark and mystical. Like hers.

Here we are on Planet Earth, two nude girls on the nudie beach, and we are lolling like sea lions. We're just a tiny little fleck of what's happening in the world. Our nudity hardly matters. In other parts of our town, the escapades are more interesting. Parents are getting divorced, derelicts are peeing on the wall of the bus station, windows are being opened to let the fall air fly in. Ma loves fall. She's big on opening the whole house up to blow Max's cologne smells out.

Here on the beach, male idiots are walking past us with their surfboards tucked underneath their wings. They're saying, Whoa.

They're saying, Hi girls.

They're not used to seeing such beauty on the sand, Blythe whispers. Honk if you believe in Jesus, she says to a group of boys jumping up and down, laughing like sand fleas, not even trying to control their joy.

I look at Blythe's face, and she looks at mine. I envy her blank eyes. There is no question in my mind that Blythe has had sex at least once. She acts a million years smarter than me, even though our birthday's the same.

A soccer mom jogs up. What the hell are you two thinking? she says, stopping her run and just standing there near our feet. My sunglasses block her energy out completely. Do you know what kind of trouble you're asking for? Mind if I ask your ages?

Blythe laughs, a terrible little snarly sound, like a baby warthog. Mind your own business, lady. And honk if you believe in Jesus.

Quite proud of herself, she rolls back over to look at me. She bats her very black lashes and giggles. Then she rolls the other way with her tits facing the sun. Once again my eyes get caught there. Her nipples look like alien ships hovering over her. She arches like a cat and flips her *fuck you* to the sky above the angry woman's face. I am too embarrassed to look, but I can feel the woman's shining rage.

Before she jogs away, she says we deserve to get severely punished. Calls us *dangerous*. Tells us that life is not as easy as we seem to think.

"Maybe even worse than you girls can imagine," she says.

As if.

Acknowledgments

I'd like to thank Cooper Renner for his keen editing eyes, and I'd like to thank Philip Rocker for giving this writer a home in which to write her stories.

112 N. Harvard Ave. #65
Claremont, CA 91711

chapbooks@bamboodartpress.com
www.bamboodartpress.com

www.ingramcontent.com/pod-product-compliance
Lightning Source LLC
Chambersburg PA
CBHW080756120626
46557CB00006B/1290